The Ghost of the

GOLDEN GATE
BRIDGE

by
Carole Marsh

What Kids Say About
Carole Marsh Mysteries . . .

"I love the real locations! Reading the book always makes me want to go and visit them all on our next family vacation. My mom says maybe, but I can't wait!"

"One day, I want to be a real kid in one of Ms. Marsh's mystery books. I think it would be fun, and I think I am a real character anyway. I filled out the application and sent it in and am keeping my fingers crossed!"

"History was not my favorite subject until I started reading Carole Marsh Mysteries. Ms. Marsh really brings history to life. Also, she leaves room for the scary and fun."

"I think Christina is so smart and brave. She is lucky to be in the mystery books because she gets to go to a lot of places. I always wonder just how much of the book is true and what is made up. Trying to figure that out is fun!"

"Grant is cool and funny! He makes me laugh a lot!"

"I like that there are boys and girls in the story of different ages. Some mysteries I outgrow, but I can always find a favorite character to identify with in these books."

"They are scary, but not too scary. They are funny. I learn a lot. There is always food which makes me hungry. I feel like I am there."

What Parents and Teachers Say about Carole Marsh Mysteries . . .

"I think kids love these books because they have such a wealth of detail. I know I learn a lot reading them! It's an engaging way to look at the history of any place or event. I always say I'm only going to read one chapter to the kids, but that never happens—it's always two or three, at least!"
—Librarian

"Reading the mystery and going on the field trip–Scavenger Hunt in hand–was the most fun our class ever had! It really brought the place and its history to life. They loved the real kids characters and all the humor. I loved seeing them learn that reading is an experience to enjoy!"
—4th grade teacher

"Carole Marsh is really on to something with these unique mysteries. They are so clever; kids want to read them all. The Teacher's Guides are chock full of activities, recipes, and additional fascinating information. My kids thought I was an expert on the subject—and with this tool, I felt like it!"
—3rd grade teacher

"My students loved writing their own Real Kids/Real Places mystery book! Ms. Marsh's reproducible guidelines are a real jewel. They learned about copyright and more & ended up with their own book they were so proud of!"
—Reading/Writing Teacher

"The kids seem very realistic—my children seemed to relate to the characters. Also, it is educational by expanding their knowledge about the famous places in the books."

"They are what children like: mysteries and adventures with children they can relate to."

"Encourages reading for pleasure."

"This series is great. It can be used for reluctant readers, and as a history supplement."

30 YEARS AGO . . .

As a mother and an author, one of the fondest periods of my life was when I decided to write mystery books for children. At this time (1979), kids were pretty much glued to the TV, something parents and teachers complained about the way they do about video games today.

I decided to set each mystery in a real place—a place kids could go and visit for themselves after reading the book. And I also used real children as characters. Usually a couple of my own children served as characters, and I had no trouble recruiting kids from the book's location to also be characters.

Also, I wanted all the kids—boys and girls of all ages—to participate in solving the mystery. And, I wanted kids to learn something as they read. Something about the history of the location. And I wanted the stories to be funny.

That formula of real+scary+smart+fun served me well. The kids and I had a great time visiting each site, and many of the events in the stories actually came out of our experiences there.

I love getting letters from teachers and parents who say they read the book with their class or child, then visited the historic site and saw all the places in the mystery for themselves. What's so great about that? What's great is that you and your children have an experience that bonds you together forever. Something you shared. Something you both cared about at the time. Something that crossed all age levels—a good story, a good scare, a good laugh!

30 years later,

Carole Marsh

Christina "Mystery Girl" Mimi Papa Grant

Hey, kids! As you see—here we are ready to embark on another of our exciting Carole Marsh Mystery adventures! You know, in "real life," I keep very close tabs on Christina, Grant, and their friends when we travel. However, in the mystery books, they always seem to slip away from Papa and me so that they can try to solve the mystery on their own!

I hope you will go to www.carolemarshmysteries.com and apply to be a character in a future mystery book! Well, the *Mystery Girl* is all tuned up and ready for "take-off!"

Gotta go...Papa says so! Wonder what I've forgotten this time?

Happy "Armchair Travel" Reading,

Mimi

Christina Grant Lily Makito
Yother Yother Johnson Nakagawa

BOUT THE
CHARACTERS

Christina Yother, 10, from Peachtree City, Georgia

Grant Yother, 7, from Peachtree City, Georgia,
Christina's brother

Lily Johnson, 10, from McDonough, Georgia, as Lynn

Makito Nakagawa, 8, from Peachtree City, Georgia, as Scott

The many places featured in the book actually exist and are worth a visit! Perhaps you could read the book and follow the trail these kids went on during their mysterious adventure!

TITLES IN THE CAROLE MARSH MYSTERIES SERIES

Books and Teacher's Guides are available at booksellers, libraries, school supply stores, museums, and many other locations!

CONTENTS

1 A Foggy Landing!

"Papa, I thought you said we were 'bringing this plane down' a few minutes ago and that we were almost to San Francisco. So why are there still clouds?" Christina asked her grandfather.

"I am bringing us down, Christina," Papa replied, as he guided his small red and white airplane into San Francisco airspace. "We're not in clouds, we're in fog. Didn't you know that San Francisco is famous for the fog that comes in from the ocean during the summer?"

"But you can't see a thing, Papa!" exclaimed Christina, brushing her long brown hair over her shoulder and rubbing her tongue over the new braces on her teeth.

1

"Maybe Papa has X-ray vision," said Grant, Christina's blond, curly-haired little brother. He pulled his blue eyes wide open with his fingers and stared at Christina.

"Stop that, Grant!" Christina ordered. "You're not helping things!"

Mimi, Christina and Grant's grandmother, sensed Christina's anxiety. "Don't worry, Christina," she said calmly. "You know that Papa is the best pilot in the whole world and the *Mystery Girl* always takes us safely wherever we want to go."

"Oh, I know," Christina said, nodding her head. "This fog just gives me a creepy feeling."

Christina and Grant often joined their grandparents on trips—all over the United States—and to other countries, too! Mimi, a children's mystery book writer, often traveled to her book locations to do research.

But this time, Mimi wanted to relax and visit with some friends, Mr. and Mrs. Chambers, in San Francisco. Plus, she knew the children would love San Francisco, one of the most exotic and exciting cities in the world! The children enjoyed traveling with

Mimi and Papa, and somehow their trips always became an adventure!

The wispy fog outside Christina's window seemed to grow thicker with each passing minute.

"When are we going to land?" she asked, her hands clenched.

Papa decided to divert Christina's attention. "Christina, listen. I have a song for you," he said.

"You do?" she asked in anticipation.

"Yep, here goes!" Papa began singing in his loudest baritone voice, "I left my heart . . . in San Francisco . . . high on a hill . . . it calls to me . . ."

Mimi beamed. "I always did like that song!" she exclaimed, patting Papa on the shoulder.

Grant interrupted Papa's serenade. "Look! I see something . . . there . . . in the fog . . . it's something red!" he exclaimed. "Is that the bridge you told us to look for?"

"Yes, that's it!" exclaimed Mimi.

"Oh, it's beautiful!" Christina said. "But the way it's mostly hidden in the fog . . . there's something sort of . . . well, mysterious about it."

4 *The Ghost of the Golden Gate Bridge*

"Oh, sweetie," Mimi said with a sigh, "remember, I'm here strictly for pleasure—I don't want to even hear the word 'mysterious' used around me this week! Okay?"

"It's awesome!" shouted Grant. "But . . . it's not gold," he added, disappointed. "I thought you said it was a *golden* bridge!"

"It's named the Golden Gate Bridge, but it's not made of gold or even painted gold," explained Mimi. "Many years ago, a man named the opening where the mouth of the San Francisco Bay meets the Pacific Ocean the 'Golden Gate.' So, when the bridge was built to cross this opening, they decided to call it the Golden Gate Bridge."

"We're here!" Christina announced, as the *Mystery Girl's* tires softly touched the runway. Papa looked at Christina and winked. "I'm glad to get out of that soup, too!" he remarked.

Papa plopped his cowboy hat on his head and reached for Mimi's hand. "Let's get out and stretch our legs, shall we?"

2 THE BRIDGE THAT COULDN'T BE BUILT

"Welcome to San Francisco!" A young boy and girl shouted the greeting as they bounded across the runway toward the *Mystery Girl*. The children were Asian, with coffee-colored skin and dark, sparkling brown eyes. The girl's long, black hair glistened in the sun. An older man and woman hurried behind them.

"What a pleasant surprise for you to meet us here!" exclaimed Mimi, as a gust of wind tipped her wide-brimmed red hat, revealing the short blond curls underneath. She turned to Christina and Grant. "This is Mr. and Mrs. Chambers and their two grandchildren!" She buried

5

Mrs. Chambers in a bear hug while Papa and Mr. Chambers shook hands and slapped each other on the back.

"Look at you!" declared Mr. Chambers as he scrutinized Papa. "Still wearing jeans, cowboy boots, and a cowboy hat, I see! But are you still the free-spirited **maverick** I once knew?" Mr. Chambers asked Papa.

"You bet!" Papa replied. "Still as untamed and free . . . just galloping a little slower is all!"

"We couldn't wait to see you!" Mrs. Chambers panted as she tried to catch her breath. "We decided to have our chauffeur, Mr. Wong, drive us all here. Plus, our grandchildren, Scott and Lynn, were anxious to meet Christina and Grant. Scott and Lynn will be staying with us this week. Oh, I've got lots of plans to keep these kids entertained!"

Scott grabbed one of Grant's bags. "Hey, come on, my grandparents have a really cool limousine!" he said. "I'll race you to the parking lot!"

"You'll like Mr. Wong," said Lynn, as she helped Christina with her rolling luggage. "He's a really nice driver. Plus, he knows just about everything about San Francisco. He and his family have lived here a long time! His wife knows lots of stories, too. She's the storyteller at the Asian Museum."

When they reached the limousine, they found a middle-aged Asian man in a black suit standing stiffly by the open trunk. Mrs. Chambers introduced Mr. Wong to everyone. He bowed and said in a slow, deliberate way, "It will be my pleasure to be your driver. Welcome to San Francisco. Is this your first time to visit our great city?"

"It's the first time for my grandchildren," said Mimi, "but Papa and I have been here before."

"Ahh, I see," answered Mr. Wong, as he turned toward the children. "Then I will be happy to give you my own special tour. My family has lived in Chinatown for generations."

Christina was puzzled. "But Lynn just said you were from San Francisco and now you are saying you're from Chinatown. I'm confused!"

"Let me explain," Mr. Wong said. "Chinatown is a section of San Francisco where thousands of Asians settled. It's like a small bit of China in America."

Mrs. Chambers said, "Mr. Wong has been with our family for many years. He is an excellent driver and a trusted friend. I've asked him to drive you and the children wherever you need to go!"

"That sounds wonderful! Thank you," replied Mimi, as she climbed into the limousine in her spiky red pumps.

Soon the black limo was cruising down the expressway toward the city. Mr. Wong drove around a rocky bend, and before them stood the first massive tower of the Golden Gate Bridge. Its bright reddish color contrasted sharply with the sparkling blue water of San Francisco Bay swirling below.

Christina and Grant gasped. "Man, that sure looks a lot bigger than it did from the airplane," Grant said.

"I didn't realize it was so tall!" exclaimed Christina.

"The Golden Gate Bridge was built over 70 years ago," Mr. Wong explained. "It is known as 'the bridge that couldn't be built' because no bridge had ever been built to cross this distance of water. It took four years to build, and today it is still one of the tallest and longest bridges in the world."

"What are those ropes for?" asked Grant, his nose pressed to the window.

"Those are steel cables, my son," Mr. Wong replied. "It is a suspension bridge. The weight of the bridge and the traffic are supported by those two gigantic steel cables you see suspended between the two towers. Smaller cables attach the road to the large cables. The large cables are three feet thick and contain enough steel wire to circle the earth three times! This bridge is well traveled each day. It's estimated that more than half a billion vehicles have crossed it over the years!"

Grant piped up, "Make that half a billion and one, now that we're crossing it!" Everyone chuckled.

"Look at all the boats!" Christina exclaimed.

"Yes," Mr. Wong continued. "San Francisco is an international port, with ships arriving from all over the world every day. When people first came to San Francisco on large clipper ships, the passengers would tear the ships apart and use the wood to build houses and stores.

San Francisco is a true 'melting pot' of people from many nationalities and cultures. We've already talked about Chinatown, but there's also Japantown and Russian Hill!"

"This place is so cool!" Grant exclaimed. "Look at those houses built into the hills!" Christina nodded in agreement.

"As we reach the end of the bridge," Mr. Wong said, "look down below the bridge and you might catch a glimpse of Fort Point. This fort was built during the Civil War to help protect the city. At first, when the bridge was being built, there were plans to tear it down. However, many people objected, so the builders changed their plans and preserved the fort. Today, it is a museum. In fact, I have a brother who worked there for many years, until recently."

Mr. Wong looked back at the children in his rearview mirror. "Oh, and speaking of family," he continued, "I almost forgot. My wife wanted me to invite you to the Asian Museum where she will be telling a story tomorrow morning. Would you like for me to drive you there?"

"Can we go, Mimi?" pleaded Christina and Grant.

"Certainly!" exclaimed Mimi. "In fact, Papa and I might go along to tour the Asian Museum. I've heard it has a remarkable collection of Asian art!"

The limousine lumbered slowly up and down the steep hills on the way to Pacific Heights, where Mimi had booked an apartment for the coming week.

3 A GHOSTLY APPEARANCE

Grant threw open the double doors to the living room of their apartment. Two plush sofas and two over-stuffed chairs surrounded a magnificent Oriental rug. Sunlight spilled in from a tall picture window partially covered by thick, red velvet drapes. Doors on either side of the living room led to two bedrooms, one for Mimi and Papa and one for Grant and Christina.

"Welcome to our 'home away from home,'" Mimi announced.

"Oh, give me a home . . . " Papa started singing, "where the buffalo roam . . . and a great view of the bridge!"

"Oh, Papa!" Christina said. "I doubt we can see the bridge from here!"

"Well, let's just see about that, young lady," Papa retorted. He marched over to the window, pulled the curtains aside, and exposed the view. "Ta dah!"

"Wow!" Christina exclaimed. "You can see everything from up here—the Golden Gate Bridge and the bay . . . it's so beautiful!" She whirled around to look at her grandfather. "Papa, you were right!" she said. "But how did you know?"

"Oh, I'm just talented that way!" he said with a big grin.

"Or," added Mimi, "I just might have told him I specifically reserved an apartment with a view of the bridge!" She lightly bumped Papa on the shoulder with her hand.

"Hey Christina," called Grant from their bedroom, "I call this bed mine!" His sister peeked in the doorway just as Grant catapulted onto the nearest twin bed.

"Oh, you mean you're 'staking your claim'?" questioned Mimi from the living room.

"What do you mean by that, Mimi?" asked Grant.

"That's a phrase they used in the old Gold Rush days," Mimi replied. "When a miner struck gold, he declared that the land around his find and underneath it was now his property. He marked the area with signs or wooden stakes and registered his claim with the local officials. Then, any more gold found in that area became his property as well."

"Tell us more about the Gold Rush, Mimi," begged Grant.

Mimi sat on the bed next to Grant and put her arm around him. "Well, it's almost time for you two to go to bed. But I can tell you that the California Gold Rush started in 1848, when gold was discovered at Sutter's Sawmill near this area. People came here by the thousands from all over the world, hoping to find gold and get rich quick!"

"Did they find it? Did they get rich?" asked Grant.

"Well, a few people did, but most of the people didn't," replied Mimi. "And now it's time for you two to go to sleep. Good night, my little travelers." She kissed each of them on the cheek.

Even though they were exhausted, sleep did not come easily for the children. Grant couldn't stop thinking about the Gold Rush. He wondered if he might find gold on this trip and stake his own claim! He even thought up a name for it. He'd call it *Grant's Goldmine!*"

Christina was thinking about gold, too, but in a different way. She wondered if she could buy a real piece of California gold jewelry as a souvenir of the trip. But, she knew it would probably be expensive. Eventually, Grant fell asleep, but Christina tossed and turned. She decided to get up and go into the living room to get one more glimpse of the bridge.

Suddenly, she saw something moving on the bridge! Was that a man? What was slung over his shoulder? Christina's eyes widened in disbelief as she saw him climb one of the suspension cables. What was he doing? Suddenly, there was a bright

and the man disappeared into the thick night fog.

Christina rubbed her eyes, thinking she was seeing things. She kept watching, hoping she would spot him again. But she never did. All she saw were trucks and cars flowing across the bridge. She suddenly felt very tired and dragged herself back to her room. *As she snuggled beneath the pink comforter, she thought, did I really see what I think I saw?*

4 A Fragile Frog

The next morning, Christina stumbled into the living room. She found Mimi sipping coffee on the sofa, and Papa settled in one of the plush chairs, reading the morning newspaper. Christina perched on one of the arms of Papa's chair and began reading over his shoulder. An article on the front page immediately caught her eye.

THE GHOST OF THE GOLDEN GATE BRIDGE RETURNS!

Christina snatched the paper out of Papa's hands. "Let me see that!" she demanded.

"Well, excuse me . . . I believe I was reading that!" countered Papa.

"No, you don't understand!" wailed Christina. "I got up last night, looked out the window, and I saw that ghost they're talking about in the paper—with my own two eyes!"

"No kidding!" said Papa, "Here, let me read it out loud, so we all can figure out what's going on."

The article quoted witnesses who saw a man with a white beard climbing up one of the cables on the bridge. They said he had a pickaxe slung across his back. Then, the witnesses reported seeing a bright flash and—

Several of the witnesses speculated that he was the ghost of an old gold miner, still prospecting for gold! Apparently, this was his second appearance.

Mimi said, "I'm just going to pretend I didn't hear any of this. After all, I am on vacation." She turned and briskly walked into her bedroom with her hands on her ears.

"But," she added, popping her head out of the bedroom door, "that is a very well written article! Who's the writer?"

"Angela Reynolds, Investigative Reporter," Papa replied.

"Nice work," Mimi remarked, closing the door.

"Hey, Christina," Grant said, rubbing his eyes as he padded into the room wearing fluffy yellow slippers. "What's a ghost's favorite pie?"

Christina took the bait. "Okay, Grant, what is it?"

"Boo Berry!" Grant exclaimed, giggling at his early-morning joke.

"Very funny!" Papa said. "Now, how about adding some berries to that cereal I set out on the table for you?"

The telephone startled Christina. Papa answered it and told the kids that Mr. Wong would be there soon to drive them to the Asian Museum.

Christina's mind raced as she got dressed. She was the first one ready.

"Mimi," she said, "I'm going to wait for Mr. Wong outside." As she opened the apartment door, a splash of bright green on the black doormat caught her eye. It was a green origami frog!

"Oh . . . how cool!" she exclaimed.

She reached down and gingerly picked it up. Mimi appeared behind her. "What's that?"

"Look, Mimi, an origami frog," Christina said. "I found it lying out here on the mat. I made one just like it in school when we were studying Asian cultures. Only the one I made didn't look as good as this one!"

"Perhaps someone dropped it," suggested Mimi. "Or, you have a secret admirer! At any rate, we all need to go downstairs . . . we don't want to keep Mr. Wong waiting." She gathered Grant and Papa and they all headed down the stairway. Christina continued inspecting the frog as she slowly followed the others. There was writing on it! It read:

When they reached the bottom of the stairs, Mr. Wong stood waiting with the limousine's doors opened wide. As Christina was about to climb in, she turned to him.

"Look, Mr. Wong," she said, showing him the frog. "I found this just now outside our apartment. What do you make of it?"

"Ahhh . . . an origami frog . . . a symbol of luck," he said.

"Really?" Christina asked. "That's good! Can you tell me what the message means?"

"Kaeru is Japanese for frog . . . but it can also mean 'to return to.' So, all together, it could mean either 'good luck to the news' or 'return to the news,'" Mr. Wong explained.

"Neither one of them makes any sense to me," Christina mumbled.

"I'm afraid I don't understand the message, either," said Mr. Wong. "Perhaps it is a riddle. At any rate, it's time we get going. The Chambers family is waiting inside the limousine." Mr. Wong motioned to the seat and Christina climbed in, mulling over the message in her mind. *What did it mean? And from where— or from whom—did it come?*

5 TALE OF TWO DIGGERS

Once they reached the Asian Museum, the adults began their tour while Mr. Wong led the four children to the storytelling room.

"Greetings!" announced Mrs. Wong. "I'm so glad to see so many children here today! Let's all sit down so we can begin. Today's story is based on an old Chinatown legend. It's called, *A Tale of Two Gold Diggers*."

Mrs. Wong settled into a sky-blue easy chair with braided gold trim. "Once upon a time," she began, "during the California Gold Rush days, there was a boy named Chin Woo. He came from China and settled in Chinatown along with his father, his mother, two younger brothers, two younger sisters, and his grandmother. However, Chin Woo hadn't seen his father for a year. He was one of many Chinese men building the Transcontinental Railroad that would connect the East Coast with San Francisco. Chin Woo cried himself to sleep many nights. He missed his father so much! He often heard his mother crying, too.

"Chin Woo's mother worked as a waitress at a Chinese restaurant called 'The Golden Lantern.' Chin Woo worked there, too. He cleared the tables, washed dishes, mopped the floor, and ran errands for the owner, Mr. Lee. You see, in those days, many children worked instead of going to school to keep food on the table. Chin Woo's grandmother took care of the younger children at home.

"One night, while Chin Woo and his mother were working at the restaurant, two dirty, bearded men burst through the front door. Chin Woo knew they were gold diggers by the miner's picks that rested on their shoulders. He also knew it was best to stay out of any gold digger's way, so he retreated to the kitchen, but peeked around the corner out of curiosity.

"Mr. Lee greeted them at the front door. He pointed to their mining picks and motioned towards the front door since he didn't speak much English. The two gold diggers looked at him for a moment, then threw back their heads and laughed heartily. One of them moved the pick in front of him, looking like he had just become armed with a weapon.

"'*Just try to take this from me, old man,*' the gold digger snarled.

"Chin Woo became frightened. He thought the gold digger might harm Mr. Lee.

"Mr. Lee took a step backward. Now he was afraid. Then, he pointed to the pick and back to the wall.

"'*Well, now, that's more like it,*' the other miner drawled.

"The men sauntered over to a table near the wall, sat down, and rested their picks against the wall next to them. Chin Woo's mother took their order without uttering a word. As she started walking back to the kitchen, she overheard one of the miners whisper to the other one, *'Don't worry, none of the people in here know English.'* (This was their first mistake, because the gold diggers didn't know that Chin Woo's mother couldn't *speak* English, but she *understood* almost everything anyone said in English.)

"When the food was ready, Chin Woo's mother silently slid the steaming plates of rice, vegetables, and shrimp in front of the men. They gobbled it up as if they hadn't eaten in a long time. After they finished their meal, Chin Woo cleared their dishes while his mother set up a table next to them. She couldn't help but overhear their hushed conversation.

"*'Hey Zeke,'* commented one miner. *'We done real good so far. We struck a vein. We made it to San Francisco with the gold. Do you think it's safe—where we hid the first batch?'*

"*'Sure, Hank,'* replied Zeke. *'Like I told ya, it's safer than any bank. There are just too many bank robberies these days. Plus, in a stronghold like that—no one will ever get to it. Trust me, it is safe and sound. You still have the key, right?'*

"*'Yeah, I've got it right here in my shirt pocket,'* answered Hank, patting his pocket.

"When Chin Woo's mother returned to the kitchen, she pulled him toward her and quietly instructed him to follow the two men when they left the restaurant.

"*'Just don't let them see you,'* she whispered. Chin Woo nodded in obedience. *'And remember,'* she added, *'be very careful!'*

"Soon, the men hoisted their picks over their shoulders. Zeke reached into his pocket, pulled out a coin, and tossed it nonchalantly in the air toward Mr. Lee.

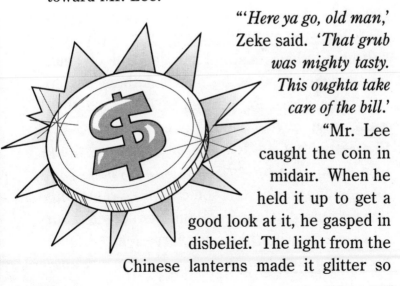

"*'Here ya go, old man,'* Zeke said. *'That grub was mighty tasty. This oughta take care of the bill.'*

"Mr. Lee caught the coin in midair. When he held it up to get a good look at it, he gasped in disbelief. The light from the Chinese lanterns made it glitter so much that even Chin Woo could see its gleam from the kitchen door. The owner wasn't holding just any coin. He was holding a genuine gold dollar!

"Wow, thought Chin Woo. That's my mother's pay for a month of work—with me helping her!

"The two miners walked out the door. Chin Woo silently slipped out the back door and into the alley. He followed them all the way to Fisherman's Wharf where the men stopped near a rickety wooden boat. Chin Woo peeked around the corner of a building to watch what they did next.

"Chin Woo noticed one small trunk in the bottom of their boat. I bet it's full of gold, he thought. Just as he watched them paddle away, the dense fog enveloped them and they were soon out of sight. He raced back to the restaurant to tell his mother everything he'd seen.

"About a week later, some lawmen came into the restaurant. Chin Woo's mother served them and overheard their conversation. They mentioned that two gold diggers were missing, and were afraid the men were either lost at sea or had come to harm. Plus, they had heard the men had no formal wills.

"Chin Woo's mother discussed this new development with her son.

"The next day, before going to work, Chin Woo walked to the harbor. The fog had cleared so he had a clear view of the sparkling bay against the blue horizon. Suddenly, he knew where the men were headed! He rushed home to tell his mother his idea.

"'*Mother, mother!*' he cried as he burst into his house. '*I know where the gold diggers went last night!*'

"'*Where?*' she asked, wiping her hands on a threadbare kitchen towel.

"'*They went to Alcatraz Island!*' Chin Woo shouted. '*I just know it! Maybe they buried the gold on the island!*'

"The next day Chin Woo and his mother rowed out to the island in a tiny, paint-chipped rowboat. They searched and dug all morning. Chin Woo decided to rest under a tree. He noticed the dirt was lumpy underneath him. It was fresh dirt! Maybe this was the hole! He called for his mother and together they dug and dug until their shovels hit something hard. It was the gold diggers' trunk!

"Chin Woo and his mother hesitated. They looked at each other. *'My child,'* his mother said nervously, *'you open it.'*

"Chin Woo cautiously grasped the lid and lifted it.

"There, before him, gleamed a mound of one-dollar gold coins, just like the one he'd seen at the restaurant! They hugged each other and shouted in excitement, *'We found it! We found it!'*

"Suddenly, Chin Woo realized something. *'Mother,'* he asked, *'where is the key and the gold they said was already hidden?'*

"They searched the island until dark, looking for the key and the gold, but never found them. They rowed back to the mainland, leaving Alcatraz Island in the eerie fog behind them.

"As for Chin Woo and his family, his father finally returned from building the railroad. They opened up their own Chinese restaurant, and Chin Woo and his mother never cried themselves to sleep again!

"There are two morals to this story. *First, never underestimate people.* They usually know more than you think. *Second, never underestimate a child.* He or she may possess a wealth of knowledge! And that is the end of my story today."

Mrs. Wong placed her hands together and bowed. The children jumped up, clapping wildly.

"Mrs. Wong," Christina asked, "Umm, I have a question. Did they ever find the key, or the other gold the miners had hidden?"

"No," Mrs. Wong replied, "Chin Woo and his family never found them. Believe me, many people have tried to solve this mystery, but no one ever has."

Mrs. Wong looked at her watch and announced, "That concludes our story hour. Thank you for coming and I hope you enjoyed it."

Christina was deep in thought as she left the storytelling room. Maybe, she thought, this mystery, which was partially solved by a child years ago, might be completely solved by a child this week! After all, Mrs. Wong said never to underestimate a child!

"Come on, Christina, you slow poke!" called Grant. "Let's go eat!"

6 A FORTHRIGHT FORTUNE

The Fog City Diner in Chinatown was packed with people, so the hostess seated the adults in one booth and the children in another one nearby. As everyone examined the menus, Christina asked the other children, "Did you like the story today?"

Scott nodded his head. "Yes, I liked it."

"Me too," said Lynn. "Didn't I tell you she was a great storyteller?"

"Yeah," added Grant, "I just wish I could go back in time and help Chin Woo find the key to unlock the place where the rest of the gold is hidden."

"Well, we can't go back in time," Christina said, "but that shouldn't stop us from trying to find the key and the remainder of the gold that Zeke and Hank left behind, should it? According to Mrs. Wong's story, it's still out there somewhere!"

"What are you saying?" asked Lynn, a bit confused.

"I'm saying," Christina replied, "that if we all put our heads together, we have as much of a chance as anyone of finding the key and the gold. After all, if a child like Chin Woo could solve the first part of the mystery, why can't we solve the remainder of it?"

"Hey, I get it," said Scott. "Your grandmother is a mystery expert and we can ask her to help us."

"No! We can't do that!" Christina exclaimed. She looked around and lowered her voice. "We can't ask her because she's on vacation. But, Grant and I have solved a few mysteries ourselves, and we've gotten pretty good at following clues, tracking down leads . . . you know, mystery stuff like that."

Lynn and Scott looked at each other in silence. Then Lynn shrugged her shoulders, and said, "Okay, why not?"

Scott spoke up, "Yeah . . . count me in, too! Except for one thing—can we have some time off from mystery solving so I can take Grant skateboarding with me one day? How about it, Grant?"

"Awesome, dude!" Grant stuck his hand up in the air to give Scott a "high five."

"Let's get started," declared Christina. "Let's see, we know from the story that the gold was locked away in a stronghold, and that a very old key out there somewhere will unlock it. Now, Lynn and Scott, do you know of a place in San Francisco that could be described as a stronghold?"

Lynn and Scott sat silent for a moment. Then Scott spoke up, "The strongest place I can think of is the old federal prison on Alcatraz Island."

"Wait a minute!" Grant objected. "Won't that be dangerous with the prisoners there?"

Scott and Lynn laughed. "What?" said Grant, a frown spreading across his brow. "What's so funny?"

"You won't have to worry about prisoners, Grant," Lynn explained, "because there haven't been prisoners there for 40 years!"

"WHEW!" Grant wiped his forehead with his hand. "That's a relief!"

"You know Alcatraz just might be the place the gold diggers talked about," continued Lynn. "After all, its nickname is 'The Rock'—that's a pretty strong-sounding name!"

"Do you think we could go there and do some investigating?" asked Christina.

"Sure," Lynn answered. "I know my grandmother planned to take your Mimi to a spa tomorrow. I'm sure our two grandpas would take us to Alcatraz, if we asked them."

"Perfect!" Christina declared. "We'll think of a way to go exploring once we get there. We're on our way to solving this mystery already!"

The waitress appeared with a massive bowl of steaming hot rice. She set it in the middle of their table. Then she placed plates heaped with

chicken, beef, and vegetables in front of each
child.   Lynn and Scott quickly grabbed the
chopsticks and dug into their lunch.

"Wow, you two are really good at using
chopsticks!" Christina declared in amazement.

"We use them all the time!" answered Scott.
"After all, our dad is Chinese-American."

Grant put a chopstick in each hand and tried
to grab a piece of grilled chicken.

It fell right back onto his plate. He tried
again. This time it fell in his lap. On his third
try, the piece of chicken came tantalizingly close
to his mouth, but jiggled and landed right in
his drink!

"I'm so hungry!" Grant wailed. "But I'm
going to starve with these stick things!"

Everyone, including the adults, broke out in laughter.

"I can teach you how to hold the sticks, Grant," offered Scott. "But let's ask the waitress for some forks, just in case."

"Thank you!" Grant replied in relief.

At the end of the meal, the waitress brought four fortune cookies. Lynn said, "Did you know that fortune cookies were invented in San Francisco many years ago, not in China?"

"Really?" commented Christina, as she cracked open the cookie to find her fortune. She was the first to read hers out loud. "Mine says,

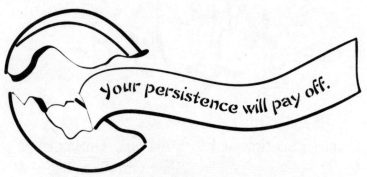

your persistence will pay off.

Next, Scott shared, "Mine says, 'Your knowledge will prove useful.'"

Then Lynn read hers, "Mine says, 'A familiar person from the past returns.'"

Champs at using chopsticks!

Finally, Grant shared, "Mine says, 'A treasure awaits your discovery.'" Grant's blue eyes lit up. "I knew it!" he cried. "I knew I would find a treasure one day soon!"

The adults gathered around the children after they finished their meal. "Mimi," Christina asked, "what did your fortune cookie say?"

"Something very odd," remarked Mimi.

"Can I see it?" asked Christina.

"Sure," Mimi replied. "It says,

Go to the stronghold.

Christina was stunned. *What could this mean? How did the person who planted Mimi's fortune know that our next move, in solving our mystery, was to find the stronghold? And why was this odd fortune given to Mimi?*

As they were leaving, Christina quietly asked the waitress, "Where do these fortune cookies come from?"

"We buy them from a bakery here in Chinatown, just down the street," whispered the waitress. "They still make all their fortune cookies by hand."

Just then, Mimi called for Christina to join them. She caught up with the group and whispered her news to the other children in the back seat of the limousine. "That's really weird," Lynn said. "Well, maybe Alcatraz really is the place!"

"Next stop, Coit Tower on Telegraph Hill," Mrs. Chambers announced, as the limousine pulled away from the restaurant.

"What's Coit Tower?" asked Christina.

"It's a major landmark of our city," Mrs. Chambers explained. "It's a tall, circular building with an incredible view of the city from the top."

"What's Tell-a-Brat Hill?" asked Grant. "Who's the brat?"

Scott and Lynn laughed. "No, Grant," Lynn said, "It's Telegraph Hill, like the telegraph machine. It's a very tall hill where a telegraph station was set up years ago. When merchant ships arrived, people on the hill spotted them and telegraphed messages to the merchants to go to the pier to get their goods. They used Morse code to telegraph messages. It uses dots and dashes for the alphabet."

"I know how to tap out my name in Morse code," Scott said. "It's fun!"

That's very nice, Christina thought, but her mind kept wandering back to the story . . . and the Ghost of the Golden Gate Bridge. Who was the ghost? Where was the key? What was the stronghold?

7 GET US OUT OF HERE!

The next morning, Papa and Mr. Chambers took the four children on the ferryboat to Alcatraz Island. The chilly bay breeze whipped through the children's hair as they huddled together in their seats.

"This place looks spooky," Christina said. "I'd hate to have to live here."

"Well," Scott said, "the people here weren't exactly nice guys, so you can't feel too sorry for them. Alcatraz Island was a good spot for a prison because it was so hard to escape from it." He pointed to the water below them. "*Freeeeezing* cold water! Sharks! Get the picture!"   Christina shuddered just thinking about it.

The group climbed off the boat and joined the line of visitors waiting to tour the prison. Suddenly, something was happening! The pot of red geraniums on the steps began to dance! The flagpole began to sway! Christina started to lose her balance! The earth was moving beneath her feet!

"What's going on?" she cried, grabbing Papa to stabilize herself.

"Hang on! It's an earth tremor!" exclaimed Mr. Chambers. And just as suddenly as it had started, the motion stopped.

"Hey, that was fun!" exclaimed Grant. "But what's an earth tremor?"

"It's when the earth moves or shakes, just slightly," explained Mr. Chambers. "San Francisco, and most of California, actually, is on the San Andreas Fault, which is a line where two of the earth's plates meet. These plates sometimes shift in position. If there's a minor movement, we experience a tremor. If there's a big movement, we have an earthquake! Earth tremors usually only last a few seconds, though."

"I'm sure glad that's over!" declared Christina. "I like my ground to stay still, thank you!"

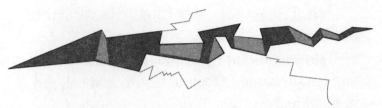

"Welcome to Alcatraz," the tour guide began, "once home to many of the most **notorious** convicts, like Al "Scarface" Capone. Only the most hard-core convicts were incarcerated here. The average prisoner stayed here five years. However, if a prisoner showed exceptionally good behavior, then he might get a **reprieve**, and be allowed to leave early."

"Gee, how would you like to live in this place for five years, Grant?" asked Scott, as he pointed to the small, barren cells.

"No way!" Grant shouted. "I'd try to get one of those reprieve things if I were stuck here."

"This place gives me the creeps," admitted Scott. He looked at his grandfather and begged, "Grandpa, would it be okay if Grant and I went outside for a little bit?"

Christina quickly spoke up. "How about if Lynn and I go with them? I have my cell phone with me."

"Well, I suppose," said Papa. He turned to Mr. Chambers. "What do you think?"

"Okay, just don't be too long, kids," Mr. Chambers warned. "Stay together, and call us if you need us."

The foursome had just stepped outside when Grant yelled, "Stop . . . I lost my shoe!"

Scott turned around, looked at Grant, and burst out laughing. "How did you lose a shoe?"

Grant stared at a gaping crack in the sidewalk. "I guess the crack ate my shoe!" he shouted. He bent down, wedged his shoe free, and declared, "Hey . . . I see something down in the dirt, at the bottom." He dug it out and uncurled his grubby fingers to show the others what he'd found.

"Grant, you found a key!" exclaimed Scott.

"Yeah," said Grant. "Or my shoe found it!"

"Could this be the key that was hidden by the gold diggers?" asked Lynn.

"I don't know, but it's worth checking out," replied Christina, examining the key from all angles. "Look, there are letters engraved on it. It says, 'U.S. GOVT.' That stands for United States Government!" Christina held the key in the air. "I have an idea!" she exclaimed. "Let's see if this key fits in any of the prison doors!"

"YEAH!" they all agreed.

The children scurried back into the prison and began trying the key in every door they came across. "Nothing works!" Scott cried. "What now?"

"Hey, why don't we try it in a cell door?" asked Grant. The group followed Grant as he wandered into a cell. He tried to slip the key into the cell door lock. It didn't fit.

"Look," said Grant, "this cell has a bed and a table with a plate and a cup." He ran his fingers along the old, rusty tin cup.

"Check out this bed," said Lynn, sitting gently on the squeaky springs.

"What's that noise?" Christina asked. "And why is that alarm ringing?"

"Hey the door's closing!" shouted Scott.

"Let's get out!" cried Lynn. Just as Scott was almost through the door, Christina pulled him back.

"You could get crushed!" she yelled, as he tumbled back inside.

"We're trapped!" exclaimed Grant.

"HELP! HELP!"

they all screamed. "Get us out of here! HELP!"

When no one answered their pleas for help, Lynn began to panic. "What are we going to do?" she asked, tears welling up in her brown eyes.

"No one is in this corridor and we could scream forever," said Christina. "Let's use our heads."

"What about your cell phone, Christina?" asked Lynn.

"Why didn't I think of that?" Christina exclaimed. She pulled it out of her pocket, flipped it open, and started to call Papa. Suddenly, she froze.

"What's the matter?" asked Lynn.

"My phone isn't getting a signal in here. It must be these thick walls," Christina answered dejectedly.

"Hey, I have an idea," said Scott. "What if I use Morse Code to tap out an S.O.S. for help?"

"Do you know the code for S.O.S.?" asked Christina.

"Sure I do," Scott responded. "I know how to tap out my name in Morse code, and my name has an 'S' and an 'O,' so it's a piece of cake!"

"But what can we use to tap out a code so that people in other parts of the prison will hear us?" asked Lynn.

Grant grabbed the cup he had been examining. "Here Scott, you can use this metal cup and tap it out on something."

"Great idea, Grant," said Scott. He frantically looked around the cell. "Hey, what if I tap it on the plumbing pipe under the sink? Then the vibration will travel through the pipe!"

"That's a great idea!" Christina said. Lynn hugged her brother in relief.

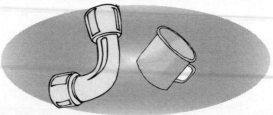

As night approached and the fog rolled in, Papa and Mr. Chambers began wondering what had happened to the children. They scoured the prison grounds for any sign of the kids.

"Now, I'm beginning to get nervous!" declared Mr. Chambers. They decided to go back into the prison and ask the tour guide to help them search for the kids inside the prison.

Papa stopped suddenly. "Listen," he whispered.

TAP. TAP. TAP.

Can you hear me?

"I hear it, too," said the tour guide.

"There's a pattern," said Mr. Chambers. A moment later he exclaimed, "It's a distress signal—S.O.S! I'll bet it's the kids!"

The three men carefully followed the sound and soon discovered the four young prisoners! The tour guide wagged his finger at them. "You children shouldn't have been in this part of the prison," he said, "but I guess I'll let you out anyway!" He quickly unlocked the door and the children came filing out one by one as quickly as they could move their feet!

As she hugged Papa's waist in relief, Christina couldn't get her mind off the key they had found. *It had to fit something . . . somewhere! But what?*

8 GOVERNMENT ISSUE

"That was a great idea to tour Fisherman's Wharf today, kids," declared Papa, as the group settled into their seats on the cable car. "It's one of my favorite spots in San Francisco."

"Mine too!" added Mimi. "I'm craving some fresh crab and a big slice of that scrumptious San Francisco sourdough bread!"

Grant and Scott wiggled in anticipation. "This cable car feels just like a ride at an amusement park!" said Grant.

"Yeah," Scott agreed, "it's always fun to ride the cable cars. We love it!"

"Who's that guy in the back holding the stick attached to the floor?" asked Grant.

"Oh, he's the grip man," said Scott. "When he moves the stick one way, it grips the cable underneath and the car rides the cable. When he moves it the other way, it releases the grip and stops the car."

"Welcome to one of San Francisco's National Historic sites . . . the cable car!" announced the conductor. "The first cable car began running in our city in the 1870s. We're very proud to continue the same safe and inexpensive service today. Our next stop is Fisherman's Wharf. If you prefer to stand, please grasp one of the overhead straps for your safety. We hope you enjoy the ride!"

The bright red cable car lurched forward. Grant thought it looked just like a single car from a passenger train, except its windows were just frames with no glass. He stuck his head out the window to feel the refreshing breeze against his cheeks. Soon, the car was slowly climbing a steep hill. As they reached the top and began their descent, the car picked up some speed.

squealed Grant as he lifted his arms to feel the wind.

"Look at those beautiful old houses," remarked Christina, gazing at the homes lining the San Francisco streets. "Some even look like castles!"

"Those are Victorian-style homes," Mrs. Chambers explained. "Unfortunately, many of the original homes were destroyed in the 1906 earthquake," she added.

"I remember hearing about a big earthquake in San Francisco at school," said Christina.

"Yes, the 1906 earthquake was one of our country's worst natural disasters," Mrs. Chambers continued. "It was so powerful that many buildings throughout the city were toppled within minutes. But the most damage came from the fires that broke out when the gas lines ruptured. The city burned for three days! Hundreds of people died and a quarter of a million people were homeless. But the people of San Francisco have a hearty spirit and were soon rebuilding again!"

"Fisherman's Wharf!" The conductor called out, as he smoothly stopped the cable car.

Christina stepped off the cable car and immediately pinched her nose. "Ooooh, what's that smell?"

"Oh, that's a mixture of fresh fish mixed with fresh sea air!" said Mr. Chambers. "See all those barrels along the street? They are full of fish or crabs. And those large black pots are where they cook the crabs or lobsters. Fish doesn't get much fresher than that!"

They meandered down the street, stopping in specialty shops along the way.   Christina thought it was almost like "going back in time," as they walked past so many old buildings. As they were walking, Christina noticed a man with a white beard across the street. *Could it be the ghost?* No, she thought. I'm grasping at straws. But seeing the man reminded her of the newly found key.

Mimi led the group into an antique shop. As the adults walked toward the back, Christina decided to seize the opportunity to find out more about the key.

"Hey, Grant," she said. "Take the key out of your pocket."

"Okay," he said. "Why?" Christina just put her finger up to her lips, signaling him to be quiet.

The children followed Christina to the counter where the shopkeeper was leafing through a magazine.

"Can I help you?" he asked.

"Yes," Christina spoke up. "My brother found this key, and we were wondering if you had seen anything like it before."

"Well, let's have a look," the shopkeeper said. He took the key and examined it closely. "I've seen a few keys like this over the years. I do know the government made this key for some government building by the inscription on it."

"How old do you think this key is?" asked Christina.

"I would speculate mid 1800s to early 1900s," said the shopkeeper.

Just then, the four adults returned from the back of the shop. "Thank you for your help," Christina said. Grant stuffed the key back into his pocket.

"How about some chocolate?" Mimi asked the kids. "You'll love our next stop!"

Mimi took the group to Ghirardelli Square, home to the famous Ghirardelli chocolate. "Try this," Mimi said, offering a square of dark, fragrant chocolate to Lynn and Christina.

"Oh, Mimi," Christina mumbled between chews, "this is yummy!" Lynn smiled, enthusiastically nodding her head in agreement.

After their chocolate snack, the group explored some of the shops on Pier 39. "Look at that two-story carousel!" Christina exclaimed. "Can we ride it, Mimi?" Mimi's nod gave the green light, and the kids raced to the carousel.

Just before they were about to board the cable car to go home, Mimi found a bakery. "Oh, I've got to take some sourdough bread home with us," Mimi said. As they opened the door and stepped inside, the smell of freshly baked bread enveloped the group.

"Ahhh . . . don't you love the smell of freshly baked bread?" asked Mimi, pinching each loaf to see which would be the tastiest.

"You'd better hurry and buy that so we can get on the cable car," Papa warned. Mimi grabbed her purchase and trotted to the cable car stop with the others. No one suspected they would soon be experiencing the ride of their lives!

9 A Mysterious Man

"Welcome to the Powell-Hyde cable car line," said the cable car operator. "In just a few minutes, you are going to have a special treat. In approximately two blocks, we will unload all passengers. Then, we will position the car on a giant turntable, where the grip man and I will show you how we manually turn the car so it can run in the opposite direction. Would anyone like to volunteer to help us turn it?"

Immediately, four small hands shot up in the air. Christina looked behind her to see if anyone else volunteered. She noticed a man wearing a hooded sweatshirt. The hood was

67

pulled down so far in front of his face that he was completely concealed.

Christina turned back around in her seat. That's odd, she thought. It's a warm day in July. Why would someone be wearing a hooded sweatshirt? And why did he pull the hood so far down over his face that he couldn't really see . . . or be seen?

"We're here," the cable car operator announced when the car reached the turntable. "Please exit the cable car and stand back. And I need my volunteers to come get their instructions," he added.

A curious thing happened next. The hooded man moved quickly down the aisle. Christina watched as he dropped something into Mimi's sourdough bread sack. Then he sprinted up the aisle and jumped off the cable car ahead of the other passengers.

Mimi grabbed the bag by one of its corners as she rose to exit the car. The weight of the bread caused the bag to tip over, and a small red object fell out. Christina quickly retrieved it. She gasped. It was a red origami bat! She turned it over and read:

This is just like the frog origami with the message on it, Christina thought. *Was this the man who left the frog on their doorstep? If so, why was he leaving these messages for Mimi?*

Just then the conductor yelled, "I need everyone off the cable car, please."

Christina clutched the note in her hand. As she joined the other kids on the sidewalk, she passed the note down to Lynn, then Scott, then to Grant. Their eyes locked. "Another piece to our puzzle," Christina whispered.

"Hope we find that safe place soon," Lynn said softly.

The conductor motioned the kids to join him. "I need the girls at the front of the cable car to stand next to me," he ordered, "and the two boys need to join the grip man at the back of the cable car."

He checked to make sure everyone was in position. "Push!" he yelled. Everyone watched in amazement as the children maneuvered the car on the turntable until it was facing the opposite direction! Mimi, Papa, and the Chambers applauded. "Hey! Look at that! Good work!" Papa shouted.

Just as everyone was preparing to get back on board, Christina noticed a woman chatting with Mimi. She wore a yellow name tag. Christina moved closer to read the tag. It said,

**Angela Reynolds
Investigative Reporter
for the
San Francisco Star**

Angela Reynolds! This must be the reporter who wrote about the Ghost of the Golden Gate Bridge, Christina thought. Her eyes widened in excitement. Then the conductor declared, "All Aboard!"

Mimi sat next to Angela Reynolds. They chatted non-stop about their favorite subject—writing! Christina and the kids discussed the message on the origami bat.

Suddenly, Papa's booming voice rang out, "HEY, BUDDY! You'd better slow this thing down!" Christina grabbed Grant and Scott on either side of her as the cable car began to speed

down another steep San Francisco hill.

The conductor didn't answer Papa. He grabbed the microphone.

"Everyone! Listen!" he shouted. "Our brakes aren't working! We'll be making an emergency stop. Bend over and put your arms on top of your head!"

Then they heard him call the central station on his radio. "Mayday, Mayday, Cable Car 73 is without brakes! I repeat—WE HAVE NO BRAKES! Send help! Mayday, Mayday! We just left Fisherman's Wharf!"

10 CABLE CAR CALAMITY

Papa turned around and yelled, "Kids! Do as he says! NOW!" Papa put one arm over Mimi's head, and one arm over his, as they both bent down in their seats.

All four children bent over and folded their arms over their heads. As they bounced up and down in the speeding cable car, Christina raised her head to see what was happening. The car was heading at full speed directly toward a park— with a curve ahead! She whispered over and over, "Oh, please make this curve. Please make this curve. PLEEEASE make this curve!"

Just then, she felt a powerful bump and the car became airborne for a moment. Christina realized they had jumped the tracks. Then she put her head down and braced for a crash.

The cable car slapped the ground and slowly slid to a stop in the grassy park.

Papa and Mimi struggled to their feet and grabbed Christina and Grant.

"Are you two all right?" Mimi asked as she held them tight. Christina could feel her grandmother shaking.

"Yes, I'm okay," Christina replied, clinging to Mimi.

Grant looked up at Papa and grinned. "That was better than a roller coaster ride!"

Papa laughed and tousled his curly hair. "Well, I can tell you right now, that's not my idea of fun," said Papa. "I'm just glad you're okay."

Mr. and Mrs. Chambers stood nearby with their arms around Scott and Lynn.

"What happened to the brakes, Grandpa?" asked Scott.

"I don't know, son," Mr. Chambers answered.

The conductor rushed over to check on them. "I am so very sorry, ladies and gentlemen," he said, wiping the sweat from his brow. "Believe me, this sort of thing has never, and I mean never, happened to us before! In fact, all of our cable cars have been recently reconditioned. The brakes are like new. I must insist that everyone go to the hospital to be checked out."

Within minutes, a bus hired by the cable car company arrived to take the group to the nearest hospital. Everyone crowded into the waiting room.

Angela slipped into a seat next to Mimi. "I really don't have time for this," she complained. "I have to get to work!"

She fidgeted for a few minutes and then hopped up to speak to the woman at the front desk. "Will you do me a favor?" she asked. "Please page my sister, Danielle Reynolds. She's a nurse on the third floor. Please ask her to come to the Emergency Room."

Angela sat back down with a huff. Christina decided to take this chance to speak to her about the ghost.

"I've been following your story about the Ghost of the Golden Gate Bridge," began Christina. "In fact, I saw him one night from our apartment's front window."

"Really!" exclaimed Angela. "I'd like hear more about what you saw . . . if it's okay with your grandmother." Just then, the elevator doors opened and Danielle rushed to her sister.

"Are you all right? What happened?" Danielle demanded. Angela stood up to talk with her. "Calm down, sis. I'm a little shaken, but that's all. The brakes on the cable car I was riding went out. But I'm fine . . . really."

"Angela!" Danielle exclaimed. "I'll bet this has something to do with that crime ring you're investigating!"

"Shhhh!" said Angela. She rose from her chair, grabbed her sister's arm, and led her to an empty corner of the room. She lowered her voice to almost a whisper. "Danielle, remember I told you that information in confidence and asked you not to discuss that with anyone."

Her sister responded loudly, "But, Angela, the brakes on your car went out just last week! This is more than coincidence! Someone is out to get you. I'm afraid that next time you won't be so lucky!"

"Don't worry, and be quiet!" Angela warned. "There's not going to be a next time. I'm being careful. Now, can you help speed things along? I'm working on a deadline here!" Eventually, all of the passengers were examined. They were sore and had a few bruises, but there were no serious injuries. Mr. Chambers called Mr. Wong to pick them up.

As Mr. Wong drove them back to their apartment, Christina reached into her pocket, searching for the origami bat. It was gone! She whispered to Grant, "Do you still have the key in your pocket? You didn't lose it, did you?"

"No," Grant replied. "It's right here—safe and sound." He patted his right thigh. "It's a good thing I have pockets that snap shut!"

Christina wondered when she would see Angela Reynolds again. If she did, she was going to tell her about the mysterious man in the hooded sweatshirt she saw on the cable car. She wondered if he was connected with the crime ring that she overheard Angela's sister mention. *Perhaps he even had something to do with the cable car accident!*

11 CRUISING IN STYLE

"I'm glad we have Mr. Wong to drive us around today," Lynn said.

"Me too," agreed Christina. "Papa said all the grandparents are just too sore from the cable car crash yesterday to go anywhere today. He said a crash like we had is harder on older folks."

Grant tried to talk through a mouthful of sticky chocolate donut. "I muth thay that going thoo the drive-thoo window of a donut thop in a limo ith a good way to thtart the day!" He swallowed and smiled, with chocolate goo covering his front teeth. "Did you see the way that lady looked at us when we drove through?" He giggled. "I thought her eyes were going to pop out of her head!"

"That was a great first choice for the day's activities, Grant," Christina observed, popping a powdered donut hole in her mouth. "Now, whose turn is it to pick where we go next?"

"Well," Lynn began, "since Grant made the first choice, how about letting a girl decide next?"

"Okay," agreed Scott. "You go next, Lynn."

Lynn was quiet for a moment. Suddenly, her sparkly brown eyes lit up. "Mr. Wong, could you please drive us to the Levi Strauss headquarters?"

"Levi's?" asked Christina. "Is that a store?"

"It's their headquarters," answered Lynn. "Levi Strauss is the man who invented blue jeans here in San Francisco during the Gold Rush days. Mr. Strauss created them as sturdy pants for gold miners. They have every jean item you can think of—at discount prices!"

"Shopping?" groaned Grant. "Do we have to go, too?"

Mr. Wong chuckled. "You boys can stay in the limousine with me while the girls shop," he offered.

"Oh, thank you!" sighed Grant in relief.

As they headed for the store, Lynn turned to Christina and asked, "Was the Ghost of the Golden Gate Bridge in the news this morning?"

"No," Christina said. "I looked all through the paper, and there was no news about the ghost. But I did find a small article that Angela wrote about the cable car crash. I cut it out to keep as a souvenir. I'll show it to you when we get back to the apartment. But, I've been meaning to tell you that another origami appeared on our doormat this morning!"

"What was it?" asked Scott.

"It was a yellow crane," replied Christina.

"Was there anything written on it?" asked Lynn.

MAY THIS CRANE BRING TSURU.

"There sure was," said Christina. She slipped the bright yellow paper crane out of her pocket. "Read this!" she said.

"What does that mean?" asked Grant.

"Let's ask Mr. Wong," said Lynn. She pushed the button to open the glass separating the chauffeur from the passengers. "Mr. Wong," she said, "Christina found an origami crane this morning. It has the word 'tsuru' on it. What does that mean?"

"Tsuru means 'healing,'" he explained. "Also, the crane is thought to have special healing power."

Mr. Wong swung the limo into a parking space. "Girls," he announced, "we have reached your shopping destination!"

After the girls jumped out, Scott reached inside a storage compartment and produced a travel-size checkers board. "I challenge you to a game of checkers!" declared Scott.

"You're on!" replied Grant. "I'm a checkers champ! Just wait and see!"

The girls returned in about an hour, each carrying a lumpy plastic sack. Mr. Wong asked them, "Did you find some jeans?"

"Did we!" replied Lynn. "We each got a pair of jeans, some skirts, and the cutest jean purses you ever saw!"

Scott couldn't resist. He mimicked his sister in a high voice, "Oh . . . we bought all this stuff and it's all soooo cute!"

Lynn nudged his arm. "Cut it out!" she warned.

"My children," asked Mr. Wong, "where would you like to go next?"

"Now, it's a boy's turn!" answered Scott. "Since I'm the only boy left, I choose Lombard Street, so that Grant and I can go skateboarding!"

"Excellent choice!" exclaimed Mr. Wong. "I may have to block traffic, but I think I can manage to do that for a short time. Next stop . . . Lombard Street!"

"What's so special about Lombard Street?" asked Grant.

"Lombard Street is known as 'the crookedest street in the world,'" Scott explained. "It's pretty steep, too! It has eight zig-zags!" Scott winked at Grant. "So, what do you say, Georgia boy? Do you have the **inclination** to go skateboarding? Get it . . . inclination?" Both boys chuckled while their sisters shook their heads. "Boys!" Christina said.

Christina and Grant were amazed when they got their first look at Lombard Street. Cars slowly moved down the street, carefully negotiating the twists and turns.

"Look at that!" Grant exclaimed. "It just zigs and zags and then zigs some more," Grant observed. "I can't wait to ride these curves!"

"Just watch me, Grant," offered Scott, as he yanked two orange skateboards out of the trunk. "The trick is you can't go too fast or you'll never make the eight turns. In fact, we may have to stop at several points to slow us down."

Scott hopped on his skateboard and handed the other one to Grant. "I'll block the street until you are done skateboarding," Mr. Wong said, as he parked the limousine at the top of Lombard Street. "But, be quick about it!"

Scott zoomed off first, while Grant followed close behind.

"Look at them," Christina said. "Those two are in skateboard heaven!"

The boys zigzagged all the way down and only had to stop four times to slow their pace. Just as they reached the bottom, Scott heard a cry from Grant.

Ready to roll!

Scott looked back to see Grant half-hidden in a massive rose bush loaded with magnificent red blooms—and plenty of thorns!

"What happened?" asked Scott.

"I'm stuck!" Grant cried. "This bush grabbed me, and won't let go!"

Scott scooted over to Grant and giggled. "Got a thorn in your side?"

"Just a few!" Grant grunted, struggling out of the bush. "But it was worth it!" He smiled and pumped his fist in the air. "That was totally awesome!"

The boys scrambled to their feet and jumped into the limousine, pumped with excitement.

"Way to go, guys!" the girls shouted. "You put on quite a show!" added Christina. "Especially you, Grant! You sure 'stuck' it out!"

"Very funny," Grant grumbled. "But when I get home, I'm going to tell my friends I skateboarded on the 'crookedest street in the world!' Except I'll warn them about some thorny bushes on the bottom!" he added, rubbing his bottom. The other children laughed.

"Now it's Christina's turn!" declared Lynn. "Where do you want to go?"

"I have a place in mind that will be KEY to our visit . . . if you catch my drift!" Christina said. She nodded at the other children and winked.

12 A CLANDESTINE ENCOUNTER

"My suggestion," Christina began, "is to go somewhere that is a 'stronghold' and a 'safe place.' I've been looking at the visitors' brochure, and I think our next stop should be the United States Mint in San Francisco."

"What's a mint?" asked Grant.

"It's where money is made. You know . . . pennies, nickels, dimes . . . , " replied Christina.

"Yeah . . . that's a great idea, Christina!" said Lynn. "I'm sure it's a very strong and safe building to keep robbers from stealing the money while it's being made."

"Plus, according to the brochure, it's a very old building," added Christina. "It just might be the place we've been looking for. I made sure that Grant brought his key this morning."

Mr. Wong interrupted Christina. "Excuse me," he said, "but do you want me to stop at this taquiero for lunch?"

"Oh, YES, please!" Lynn and Scott exclaimed. Christina and Grant squinted their eyes at each other. "First, tell us what a taquiero is before we agree to eat there," Christina said.

"A taquiero is a small Mexican food stand," Lynn explained. "Do you like tacos?"

"Are you kidding?" cried Grant, always eager for his next meal. "Taco is my middle name!"

Mr. Wong pulled the limousine next to the stand and ordered tacos, burritos, and nachos.

"Mmmmm," Christina mumbled after her first bite. Grant nodded approvingly, red taco sauce running down his chin.

Mr. Wong led the children into the U.S. Mint. He said, "I believe your grandparents would approve of this place . . . it's certainly educational."

They each emptied their pockets into small plastic bowls before walking through a metal detector. "Wow," commented Scott, as he eyed the security guards standing at the door. "You weren't kidding when you said that this place is safe, Christina."

A tour guide motioned them to join his group. Mr. Wong told them to follow the guide. "I'll wait for you here at the entrance until you're finished."

The children obediently followed the tour guide until they were out of Mr. Wong's sight. Then Christina spotted an alcove and motioned the other children to follow her. They hid there until the tour group ambled down the hall and turned the corner.

"Now, let's see if we can test Grant's key on some of the doors in here," Christina suggested. She led them to a storage room door nearby.

"Not going to happen," Scott said. The door had a state of the art lock on it, the kind where you slide a card into it and a green light blinks before it opens. "This place may be old," he added, "but these locks are all new. There's no way Grant's key is going to fit here."

"I guess this is a waste of our time," Christina said with disappointment as they shuffled back down the hallway. Suddenly, Christina stopped.

"Hey, there's Angela Reynolds, the reporter!" shouted Christina.

Angela turned and waved to the children. "Hello! How are you guys?"

"We're fine," said Christina. "What are you doing here?"

"Oh, just 'nosing' around for some news, as usual," Angela replied. "Where are your grandparents?"

"They're not with us today," Lynn explained. "Mr. Wong, our chauffeur, drove us here and is waiting at the entrance."

Just then, a man with a news badge walked up to Angela and whispered in her ear. "Oh . . . kids, I'd love to chat," said Angela, "but I have to go. Enjoy the rest of your visit!" She turned and quickly followed the man down the hall, her high heels clicking across the smooth floor.

The coast is clear!

Christina suddenly had a thought. "Hey guys, you know how that first origami frog message said to 'return to the news,' so I've been following the news each day?"

"Yes," replied the children.

"Well," Christina offered, "if we follow Angela, we'll be following the news because she's the one who follows the news, then writes about it. How about we do our 'spy thing' and follow her?"

"OK!" the kids shouted.

13 FOUR SPIES

The children quietly tiptoed down the hallway, following Angela. "Let's hide behind here," Christina whispered, ducking behind a massive coin display. Suddenly, they saw two men with bulging muscles walk up to Angela from behind and grab her roughly by the elbows.

"Look!" cried Scott. "She's trying to get away from them!"

"Oh, my!" gasped Christina.

When Angela's newsman companion tried to free her, two more muscle-bound men grabbed him, too. They pushed and pulled their captives through the rear exit and slammed the door behind them.

"What should we do?" asked Lynn.

"I think we should tell the security guards," said Scott.

"Yes," agreed Christina. "Come on."

Christina rushed up to a security guard in a gray uniform. "Sir," said Christina. "We just saw four really big guys take the news crew away. We think they've been kidnapped! Can you help them?"

"You're blocking the exit," the guard barked. "Get moving, kids."

"But mister . . . , " pleaded Lynn.

"I said get moving, kids! Don't you understand English?" the guard yelled.

The children raced over to Mr. Wong. "We're ready to go—now!" Christina said. As they hurried out of the Mint, Grant turned to Christina and asked, "What are we going to do? They wouldn't listen to us."

"I'm not giving up," Christina said. "Let's get outside; maybe we'll see them!"

"Look!" Scott exclaimed, pointing at an armored truck as it turned onto the street in front of the Mint and sped directly past them.

"Hey, those are the guys who grabbed Angela!" exclaimed Christina.

Follow that truck!

"Hey, Mr. Wong," said Scott. "Can you take us that way? And fast?" He pointed in the direction of the truck.

"Sure," said Mr. Wong.

The kids quickly scrambled into the limo.

"Uh . . . Mr. Wong," Lynn spoke up, "we'll tell you where we want to go as we go . . . okay? It's a surprise where we're heading. And, could you please step on it, Mr. Wong?"

"Okay," Mr. Wong replied. "Just give me enough advance notice to signal a turn, please."

Lynn raised the privacy glass so the kids could talk without Mr. Wong hearing them. "We'd better not tell Mr. Wong we're following some men who kidnapped the news crew—he'll take us straight home for sure," Lynn said.

"Yes, and if we call 911, chances are the police won't believe us, just like that guard," said Scott.

The black limo followed the truck through the late afternoon traffic as the fog started to roll in. They realized it was headed for the Golden Gate Bridge. Just before they reached the bridge, the truck veered sharply to the right.

"Mr. Wong . . . go right!" insisted Scott. Mr. Wong made a sharp right turn. A massive brick building loomed before them.

"What is this place?" asked Grant.

"This is Fort Point," explained Lynn. "Remember? Mr. Wong pointed it out when we drove you from the airport when you first came to San Francisco."

"Fort Point . . . , " Christina repeated. "How old is this building?"

"My grandpa said it was built around the time of the Civil War," Scott replied.

"I can't believe this!" Christina exclaimed. "I'll bet this is it! Look at it. It's old, it's the ultimate stronghold, and there is nothing safer than a fort!"

"You mean you think this is where the gold diggers . . . , " began Lynn.

"That's exactly what I'm saying!" interrupted Christina.

Just then, the armored truck disappeared behind the back of the building.

"Uh . . . Mr. Wong, can you park right here in the parking lot?" asked Lynn.

"Certainly, my children," he replied. "Why didn't you tell me you wanted to go to Fort

Point? I see it's almost closing time. Do you have enough money to go inside?"

"Yes . . . we do." Lynn spoke for the group.

"The fog's coming in so don't be too long," warned Mr. Wong. "I'll stay right here at this spot so you'll know where to find me. I'm a bit tired. I think I'll just rest here."

"Okay," the kids replied. They hopped out of the limousine and headed for the fort. Mr. Wong pulled his cap over his eyes and settled in for a short nap. He didn't see the children turn as they reached the front entrance and race to the back of the building.

The children peeked around the corner just as the four men finished locking the steel basement door. They heard one of the men say, "They'll be safe in this hole until Big Al comes. No one can even hear them if they scream!" Then they slapped each other on the back and laughed heartily. "Let's get out of here."

"Oops, they're coming back our way," whispered Christina. "Everyone, quick, duck under these bushes!"

14 TO THE RESCUE!

The four children quickly hid behind a hedge of thick bushes. The men walked right by without noticing them. Once the men climbed into their truck and drove away in the wispy fog, the children popped up and ran as fast as they could to the basement door. They heard faint, muffled noises.

"It's a steel door! What can we do?" asked Lynn.

"Let's go alert someone inside the museum," Christina suggested. "Maybe they have a key!" She took a few steps back toward the front of the building.

Grant stopped her. "Wait!" he shouted. "What about my key?"

"Hey, this is an old building!" Scott said. "Give it a try, Grant."

Grant yanked the key from his pocket. His hand shook as he tried to slide it into the lock. It wouldn't go in.

"Try it the other way," suggested Christina.

Grant turned the key upside down, inserted it, and the tumblers clicked! It worked!

"He did it!" exclaimed Scott. "He unlocked the door!"

Christina was the first to rush inside. "Angela . . . it's me, Christina! We're here to help you!"

Angela rushed to Christina and wrapped her in a warm hug. "Thank goodness you're here!" she said. "How did you find us?"

"I don't know who you are," said the other newsman, "but I've never been so glad to see anyone in my life!"

"Oh, kids," Angela said, "this is Tom Dawkins, our staff photographer. And Tom, this is Christina, Grant, Scott, and Lynn. I met them all on my recent cable car escapade."

"Very glad to meet you," said Tom, as he shook their hands.

"Look at this place!" exclaimed Lynn, as she and Grant ventured further into the damp, dark basement.

"Hey everyone . . . over here!" shouted Grant, pointing at the dirt floor. "Those are two miner's picks. Could they be the gold diggers' picks?"

Christina leaned over to examine Grant's discovery.

"Look!" Grant continued. "The picks form an X. Just like 'X marks the spot' . . . like on a pirate's treasure map."

Everyone was silent for a moment. "Well, what are we waiting for?" said Scott. "Let's start digging!" He grabbed a pick and began stabbing at the dirt floor.

"Uh, hmmm," Angela cleared her throat. "I hate to interrupt, but we need to get out of here! Those guys talked about bringing their buddy Al to visit us, remember?"

Christina knew she had to explain what the kids were doing. "Angela," she said, "we recently heard Mrs. Wong, a storyteller at the Asian Museum, tell a story about two gold diggers who hid a chest of gold coins. Are you familiar with the story?"

"Sure," replied Angela, tapping her foot impatiently. "It's a regular urban legend."

"Well, maybe not," Christina continued, holding up Grant's key. "Grant found this key in a crack on Alcatraz Island. We used that key to get into this basement."

"So you think that's the key from the gold digger story?" asked Angela.

"Well . . . if it is, then there's a good chance there's gold buried in here somewhere," Christina replied.

"Yeah!" Grant shouted. "And everyone knows X always marks the spot!"

"Well . . . guys . . . ," said Angela, looking at the picks and then back at the basement door. "What are we waiting for . . . keep digging! I'll keep on the lookout for Big Al—whoever that is."

15 EUREKA!

Tom and Scott were beginning to work up a sweat when the heard a loud

Everyone gathered around as Tom and Scott brushed away the dirt, exposing a small, rusted, metal trunk. They groaned as they hoisted it out of the hole. "This thing's heavy!" Tom said with a grunt.

"Why don't we let Grant do the honors?" suggested Scott, as he backed away. Grant kneeled next to the trunk, lifted the clasp, and opened it. Everyone gasped! Glinting in the dim light from the basement door was a huge pile of gold dollar coins!

Grant leaped into the air, pumping his fist. "It's the gold!" he cried. "We found the treasure! We've struck gold! EUREKA!" Then all four of the children grabbed hold of each other and jumped up and down chanting, "We did it! We did it! We solved the mystery!"

Suddenly, a massive shadow blocked the rays of sun coming through the door. A deep voice greeted them. "Well, well . . . what do we have here?"

Everyone looked up in surprise! The man had Angela by the arm.

"Who are you?" asked Christina.

"I'm Al. Who are you?" the man replied.

"I knew we should have gotten out of here!" Angela said.

Big Al crumbled to the floor. A man with a white beard and a shovel in his hand appeared behind him in the doorway. Christina gasped. *Was it the ghost?*

"You can all come out now," he said. "It's safe."

"Who are you?" asked Angela.

"I'm glad to finally meet you," said the man, nodding at Angela's nametag. Then he did something shocking—he reached up at his white beard and pulled it off! Christina gasped again. A fake beard!

"Allow me to introduce myself," he said. "I am the Ghost of the Golden Gate Bridge. Yes, I'm the one you've been writing about. My real name is Tang Wong."

"We know you!" cried Lynn. "You're Mr. Wong's cousin who worked here at the Fort Point Museum!"

Tang nodded.

"You . . . you're the ghost?" Angela sputtered in disbelief.

Just then, two police cars swerved across the gravel. Four officers jumped out.

"Boy, am I glad you're here! Who called you?" asked Angela.

"Our dispatcher got a call from a museum guard saying that someone was breaking into the back of the fort," replied one of the officers.

"Look who we have here, Sergeant," another officer said. "If it isn't Big Al!"

"Well, well, well," said the sergeant. "We've been trying to nab this guy for a long time!"

"Well, he's all yours now," replied Angela. "Oh, by the way, I am Angela Reynolds, Investigative Reporter for the San Francisco Sun. And this is my staff photographer, Tom Dawkins. We were investigating a tip we got concerning some smuggling suspected at the San Francisco Mint. Tom and I were there on assignment when four of Big Al's friends kidnapped us and locked us down here in the basement."

She looked at Al, starting to move on the floor. "I guess he didn't want to be identified in my story as head of the smuggling ring so he kidnapped us!" she explained.

"Ohhh. . . , " Al moaned, grabbing his head. "I just wanted to talk to that nosy reporter and tell her to stop snooping around the mint," he said. "I'm innocent, I tell ya!"

"We'll talk about that downtown," the policemen said. "Miss Reynolds, continue your story about what happened, please."

"Well," Angela continued, "these four children apparently followed us and came to our rescue. Then, this man here," she added, pointing to Tang, "knocked out Big Al with a shovel."

"Well, this is our lucky day!" the sergeant exclaimed. Seeing the fake beard in Tang's hand, he added, "Are you the guy who's been causing such a commotion by jumping around the Golden Gate Bridge at night?"

"Yes, I am," admitted Tang.

The sergeant spoke to Tang in a stern voice. "Under different circumstances, we would be hauling you in for disturbing the peace. But since you helped us capture Big Al, let's just call it even . . . IF you stop this crazy 'ghost' business!"

"Yes, sir, I've accomplished what I set out to do," Tang said. "The ghost will never appear again."

Grant couldn't hold in his excitement any longer. "And look what we found! It's a treasure chest full of gold coins!"

"Wow!" the sergeant exclaimed. "We may have to speak to someone in the museum about your find."

"Why?" Grant asked. "We found it . . . isn't it ours to keep?"

"Son, I'm sorry," explained one of the officers. "But we will have to establish ownership. Since it is on museum property, we'll have to discuss this with the museum."

"Ohhhh . . . ," Big Al began moaning again.

"Guess we better get this guy on his feet and take him downtown," the sergeant suggested. Two of the policemen grabbed Big Al and escorted him to the squad car.

As the group watched them leave, a man in a suit walked around the corner of the building, followed by Mr. Wong. "Children! Tang! What's going on?" Mr. Wong cried.

"Just a moment," the man in the suit said to Mr. Wong. Then he turned to the policemen. "I am Mr. Perry, the museum director," he explained. "The security guard notified me of trouble here. Is everything all right, officers?"

The sergeant explained the situation, assuring Mr. Perry and Mr. Wong that everything was under control. Mr. Perry looked at Tang and said, "Tang, what are you doing here?"

"I found this man holding these people hostage, and I struck him with a shovel," Tang explained. He turned to the children and Angela. "You see," he said, "I was employed at the Fort Museum, but they laid me off because fewer visitors visited the museum this year than last year. I know that high gas prices have affected lots of tourist destinations."

Tang held up the white beard in his hand. "I came up with an idea to bring more attention to the fort so more visitors would come see it," he explained. "So, I became the Ghost of the Golden Gate Bridge! I thought if I could capture enough attention by being a ghost, the Fort would get some publicity, then maybe more people would visit it and I would get my job back. Thanks to Angela, I was front-page news with the San Francisco Star. At least I got her attention!"

Tang looked at Christina and continued. "Then I found out from my cousin that the children's mystery writer Carole Marsh was in town. I thought she might even write a book about the fort, and make it more famous. I followed my cousin as he chauffeured you around," he said. "I left those origami messages, trying to steer Ms. Marsh to read about the ghost in the news and to the 'strong, safe' fort."

"Now, what did you find down here . . . did someone say you found gold?" asked Mr. Perry.

"Yes," replied Christina. "My brother, Grant, found this key on Alcatraz Island. We thought it might be the key that some gold diggers left many years ago—in the story of Chin Woo. Are you familiar with that story?"

"Most certainly," replied Mr. Perry, "but we have a statement of jurisdiction that any valuable historical item on our property belongs to the museum."

"Oh . . . ," said Grant, more than a little disappointed.

"Let's go to my office and discuss this situation," Mr. Perry suggested. "I can get you all something to drink."

As the group walked back to the museum entrance, Christina had some questions for Tang.

"What about that day on the cable car?" Christina asked. "Were you the man in the hooded sweatshirt?"

"Yes, that was me," Tang replied.

"Did you damage the brakes in the cable car, too?" Christina asked.

"No," Tang answered, shaking his head, "that wasn't me."

Angela turned around when she heard them talk about the brakes in the cable car. "I think it was probably Big Al and his friends," she suggested. She stuck out her right hand to shake Tang's hand. "On behalf of all of us, thank you for saving our lives."

Angela quickly got back to business. "Now, I have a few questions myself," she said. "What's with all the

FLASH

business each time you appeared as the ghost? How did you make that happen?"

"Oh, that was easy," Tang explained. "I am a trained Ninja. I have a special powder that I use to create a bright flash."

"So, that explains how you were so agile and easily eluded everyone!" Angela observed.

Mr. Perry stopped to hold the door open for everyone to enter his office. "Tang," he said, "you did all this just to gain publicity to promote the Fort?"

"Yes, sir, I did," Tang replied, hanging his head. "I wanted my job back so badly, I was willing to take some risks."

"Well, I believe I can speak for the Board of Directors when I say that you've certainly gone above and beyond the call of duty today," exclaimed Mr. Perry. "And you can have your old job back—starting tomorrow!"

16 NEVER UNDERESTIMATE A CHILD

Grant tugged at his white buttoned shirt and navy blue bow tie. "Why do I have to wear this?" he whined. "I feel like I'm being strangled!"

"Now, Grant," chided Mimi, "it's not every day that you're honored at a Museum Board luncheon! You want to look your best, don't you?"

"Yes, I guess so," Grant agreed. Then he hung his head and tugged on Mimi's shirt. He pulled her down to his level and whispered, "What I'd really like is to be able to keep the treasure that I found."

Mimi smiled. "I know, Grant, I know."

Just then, Tom asked all the guests of honor to assemble in the parlor of Mr. Perry's stately Victorian home for photographs.

"Say cheese!" instructed Angela, as Tom snapped a picture of Christina, Grant, Scott, Lynn, Angela, Mr. Wong, Tang, and Mr. Perry.

"This story is *really* going to sell papers!" exclaimed Angela. "It's about four kids who solve a mystery that's over 100 years old and how they discovered gold treasure! It's about a kidnapping, kids coming to the rescue, and how a hardened criminal was captured! And it's about how one man got his job back by being a local hero! Gosh, I might even get a bonus for this story!"

"And don't forget," added Mr. Perry, "it's also about how important our museums are and how people should visit them in every city!"

He took a box from his aide. "I have a few gifts for you children, in appreciation for your incredible discovery that will greatly benefit our museum." First, he handed Christina and Lynn tiny boxes and motioned them to open them. They both giggled and tore the paper off in just a few seconds. "These are genuine gold charm replicas of the Golden Gate Bridge." Mr. Perry explained.

"How did you know that I really wanted some gold jewelry from San Francisco? I love it!" exclaimed Christina.

Next, Scott and Grant opened their gifts— small, wooden treasure boxes with gold trim. The boys were thrilled! "A treasure box!" Grant shouted. "I finally got my own treasure box!"

"These are not just any old treasure boxes," Mr. Perry explained. "They are genuine replicas of 17th century treasure boxes seen in San Francisco many years ago! I hope you will 'treasure' them! Now, everyone please join me in the dining room for lunch."

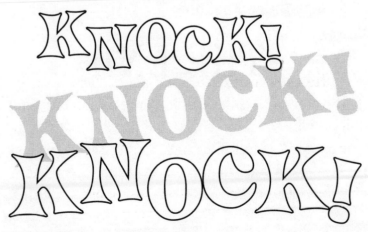

"What is that?" asked Christina, craning her neck to look at the ceiling. "It's coming from up there!"

Mr. Perry just waved his hand in the air. "Oh," he replied, "that's probably the 'ghost' that shows up every now and then. This house has been in my family for three generations, and we've always heard strange noises here. Don't worry. I'm sure it's a friendly ghost! Let's enjoy our lunch."

Christina looked at Mimi and giggled. "Don't even think about it, Christina," warned Mimi. "At least not until lunch is over!"

Everyone laughed.

"I've had enough of all this ghost business," proclaimed Grant, planting his hands firmly on his hips. "Can I eat now?"

THE END

About the Author

Carole Marsh is an author and publisher who has written many works of fiction and non-fiction for young readers. She travels throughout the United States and around the world to research her books. In 1979 Carole Marsh was named Communicator of the Year for her corporate communications work with major national and international corporations.

Marsh is the founder and CEO of Gallopade International, established in 1979. Today, Gallopade International is widely recognized as a leading source of educational materials for every state and many countries. Marsh and Gallopade were recipients of the 2004 Teachers' Choice Award. Marsh has written more than 50 Carole Marsh Mysteries™. In 2007, she was named Georgia Author of the Year. Years ago, her children, Michele and Michael, were the original characters in her mystery books. Today, they continue the Carole Marsh Books tradition by working at Gallopade. By adding grandchildren Grant and Christina as new mystery characters, she has continued the tradition for a third generation.

Ms. Marsh welcomes correspondence from her readers. You can e-mail her at fanclub@gallopade.com, visit carolemarshmysteries.com, or write to her in care of Gallopade International, P.O. Box 2779, Peachtree City, Georgia, 30269 USA.

Built-In Book Club

Talk About It!

1. How would you react if you saw something moving on a bridge in the middle of the night? What would you do?

2. Who is your favorite character in the book? Why? Which character is most like you?

3. Grant and Christina visited many places in San Francisco. Which one of those places would you most like to visit? Why?

4. Mr. Wong drove Grant, Christina, Lynn, and Scott around in a limousine. Have you ever taken a ride in a limousine? If so, where did you go?

5. Grant and Scott rode down Lombard Street on skateboards. Have you ever done an

exciting and adventurous activity like that? If
so, what did you do?

6. What was your favorite part of the
book? Why was that part your favorite?

7. Grant and Christina used Morse code
for help. Have you ever used Morse code or
any other signal to contact someone else? If so,
what did you use?

8. San Francisco has a lot of fog! Have
you ever been in fog so thick you could not see
anything around you? If so, how did that make
you feel?

9. It was frightening when the brakes on
the cable car suddenly stopped working. Have
you ever been in a scary situation like that?

10. Mr. Wong's brother dressed up like the
Ghost of the Golden Gate Bridge to get his job
back. Do you think that was a very good idea?
Did it work?

Built-In Book Club

Bring It to Life!

1. Origami can have many different meanings, depending on the shape of the origami. Look up the different meanings of origami on the Internet. Find an origami shape that you like. Create that piece of origami and present it to your book club.

2. Create a treasure chest out of a shoebox or another box and put special things in it! Hide it in a secret place, like in your closet, under your bed, or in another special place. Present a list of possible hiding places to your book club. See if anyone can guess where you hid your chest!

3. Have a Chinese feast during your book club meeting! Ask parents to help you make a Chinese dish or order some items from a Chinese restaurant. Get some chopsticks! Tell everyone that they must eat their food with chopsticks, or at least try!

4. How far are you from San Francisco? Use the Internet to find out how far away San Francisco is from your town. Then, draw a map of the United States on a piece of poster board. Draw a line from your town to San Francisco. Write the mileage above the line. Would you like to drive there or fly there on an airplane?

5. Create your own newspaper! Pretend you are a newspaper reporter. Write a news account of an earthquake in San Francisco. Explain what happened, and then write another story about how the people joined together to rebuild the city after the quake.

Glossary

agile: quick and well coordinated

anxiety: a feeling of nervousness or dread

 clandestine: something done in secret to create a diversion and throw people off

escapade: a reckless adventure or wild prank

incarcerate: to put in prison

inclination: a tendency toward a certain condition or thing, or a bending forward, tilt

 inscription: something written on a hard surface

 maverick: someone who is independent in behavior and thought

notorious: widely known for a bad reason

persistence: to continually work hard until a goal is achieved

 reprieve: a postponement of or release from a sentence handed down for a crime

San Francisco Trivia

1. Levi Strauss invented denim jeans in San Francisco during the Gold Rush. He created them for the miners who needed tough, comfortable clothing.

2. The last prisoners on Alcatraz Island were released on March 21, 1963. Alcatraz means "pelican" in Spanish.

3. Cable cars are the only moving National Historic Landmark. About 10 million people ride the cars every year!

4. The first fortune cookie was baked in San Francisco at the Japanese Tea Garden.

5. The Golden Gate Bridge has been closed three times due to high winds around 70 mph—in December of 1951, 1982, and 1983.

6. America's first Chinese immigrants arrived in San Francisco in 1848.

7. San Francisco is known for tart, crusty sourdough bread, created by French baker Isidore Boudin during the Gold Rush.

8. During the summer, the infamous fog has been known to linger on the shore for days!

9. San Francisco is one of the most popular tourist destinations in the United States. Over 17 million people visit the city every year!

10. The original Spanish name for San Francisco was *Yerba Buena*. It means "good herb."

Scavenger Hunt

Want to have some fun? Let's go on a scavenger hunt! See if you can find the items below related to the mystery. (*Teachers: You have permission to reproduce this page for your students.*)

1. ___ A picture of a cable car

2. ___ A map of California

3. ___ A pair of chopsticks

4. ___ A pair of blue jeans

5. ___ Some sourdough bread

6. ___ A piece of chocolate

7. ___ A key

8. ___ A skateboard

9. ___ A fortune cookie

10. ___ A shovel

Pop Quiz

1. What item did Grant find in the crack in the ground at Alcatraz?

2. Which character was leaving the origami messages?

3. How did Grant, Christina, Lynn, and Scott escape from the jail cell at Alcatraz?

4. True or False? Grant's key opened the door at Fort Point.

5. Where did Mimi first meet Angela Reynolds, the reporter?

6. What reward did the girls receive for helping find Big Al?

7. Where did the kids find Angela Reynolds and the treasure?

8. Where were the kids when they felt an earth tremor?

Enjoy this exciting excerpt from

THE MYSTERY OF THE HAUNTED GHOST TOWN

1 BITING THE DUST

"Ghost towns! Are we going to see real ghost towns?" Grant asked his grandfather, Papa. "And REAL ghosts in the ghost towns?"

"Could be," replied Papa, as he checked the gages of his little red and white airplane, the *Mystery Girl*, preparing the plane for landing.

"Grant, there ARE no ghosts in ghost towns!" his sister, Christina, claimed in an older-sister, bossy way, as she tugged one of his blond curls. "I told you that! Papa, you're just leading Grant on!"

"Don't be too sure about that, Christina," Papa answered, with a twinkle in his eye. "I've been in ghost towns, and I'd swear I came across a ghost or two! Those towns just might be haunted." He laughed and added, "You'll see for yourself!"

"You'll have to make a believer out of me!" Christina declared, her arms thrust across her chest.

She thought visiting ghost towns would be exciting, but certainly not scary. Sitting silently, her finger twirling a lock of her brown hair and her tongue toying with the braces on her teeth, Christina wondered if Papa was right. She suspected he would tease her in some ghost town, probably acting like a ghost to scare her, just to prove his point. I'll have to keep an eye on him, Christina thought.

Christina and Grant often traveled with their grandparents. Their grandmother, Mimi, wrote mysteries for children, and often needed to do research in fascinating locations around the world. This trip, however, was a vacation. "There are no mysteries on my agenda, thank you very much!" Mimi had said when she invited the kids to come along.

Papa knew a lot about the Old West, and was something of a cowboy, always wearing jeans, a cowboy hat, and cowboy boots. With his stories of the Old West, Papa had no trouble convincing the kids to take this vacation in southern Arizona. They had looked forward to this trip for a long time, and now the day had finally come!

Mimi was not as thrilled. There was all that heat! And sun! And dust! She loved wearing hats and sparkly red sunglasses, and now had a good reason to wear them both—to protect her blond hair and fair skin from the blazing sun!

What Mimi did love was the scenery of the West. The stark desert, with its prickly cacti and multi-colored sunsets, stole her heart every time she saw it. Plus, she couldn't wait to get her hands on the stunning pieces of jewelry handcrafted by the Native Americans!

The *Mystery Girl* slowly descended to land at a local airport near Tombstone, Arizona. The plane was now low enough so the kids could see details on the ground below.

Christina gazed out the window on her side of the plane. Immediately below, there was nothing but dry and dusty yellow land, covered in spots by some low, drab shrub brush. Here and there, tumbleweeds lazily drifted in the sandy soil.

Grant's blue eyes popped open wide. "Is that Boot Hill Cemetery over there?" he yelled, jabbing his finger against the window on his side of the plane.

"Sure is," Papa said. "That's the real thing!"

"Wow—that's where the gunslingers are buried! Can we go there, Papa?" Grant asked, jumping up and down in his seat despite being **constrained** by his seat belt.

"It's just a bunch of tombstones," Christina remarked. She thought her little brother was silly to get so excited over an old cemetery. "You can see tombstones anywhere."

"Not like those," Papa said, with another of those twinkles in his eye. "You'll see!"

"OK, Papa...I suppose ghosts pop out from behind the tombstones and talk to you," Christina said. "Can't wait to see that!" She glanced out the

window again to see a cloud of dust envelop the plane. Pebbles from the dirt runway rocketed everywhere, pelting the plane as it touched down.

Against the backdrop of the coffee-colored soil, Christina spotted a dark brown steer struggling to stand. Each time it got up, the bull collapsed again in a cloud of dust. The animal's legs were too weak for it to stand. A flock of buzzards slowly circled overhead.

Christina couldn't imagine a more **desolate** scene. She felt goose bumps on her neck. Maybe it wasn't just the ghost towns that were haunted, she thought. Maybe the whole place was haunted!

Little did she know how scary things could get in a ghost town—and a cemetery! This steer in distress was just the beginning of an Old West mystery!

Enjoy this exciting excerpt from

THE MYSTERY IN LAS VEGAS

1 TIGER TRICKS

As an eerie green glow began to illuminate the stage, Christina watched a ghostly white fog roll toward her. The soft music was growing louder. Christina could not only hear it, she could feel it rumbling in her chest.

Suddenly, ice-blue eyes pierced the mist like blazing sapphires, burning a path for two slinking tigers. Completely white except for their black stripes, they looked more phantom than feline. Christina's younger brother, Grant, yelped. "You pinched my arm!"

"Sorry," Christina mumbled, "I thought it was the chair's arm!" She brushed her long brown hair over her shoulders and settled back into her seat.

Christina knew this was only a rehearsal for the Mysteries Hotel Magic Show, but she couldn't help gripping the arms of her front-row seat in the darkness. This was her first trip to Las Vegas and it was exciting!

The owner of the hotel, Mr. Jenkins, was a friend of Christina and Grant's grandfather, Papa. Mr. Jenkins invited them to see the magic show rehearsal the minute they arrived at the hotel. They hadn't even been to their rooms yet!

Christina jumped as a booming voice announced, "Rescued from the jungles of India, they've come to share their magic with you! Ladies and gentlemen, meet the world's most regal and rare twins—Soman and Shiba!"

"Those are the most beautiful creatures I've ever seen," Christina said.

Grant's jaw dropped open as he watched the stage through binoculars. "W-w-wow," he stuttered.

"My turn," declared Mimi, the children's grandmother, peeking through Grant's binoculars. "Oh, my," she added, "they are just magnificent!"

"Look!" Grant whispered to Christina, as a girl and boy entered from each side of the stage to meet the tigers. "They're just kids!"

Spotlights focused on two large, mirrored, rotating globes that shot spears of pink light into the dark auditorium. The boy and girl commanded Soman and Shiba to jump onto the globes.

"And now," the announcer continued, "the only one these royal tigers bow to—the Maharaja of Magic, Manendra!"

Out walked a man in a sparkling blue costume and jeweled turban. Soman and Shiba changed from calm tigers to hissing, swatting beasts as he approached.

Manendra thrust his hands into the air and the fog crept back across the stage. Christina noticed two silver rings floating from the ceiling toward each of the tigers.

"I don't see any wires!" Grant exclaimed. "Do you see wires, Christina?"

As the rings neared the tigers, the music grew louder and a puff of silver smoke shot out of the globes where the tigers sat. The music stopped suddenly and the rings hit the floor with a thud. The tigers were gone!

"How'd they do that?" Grant said, clapping.

"Magic," Mimi answered.

When the music started again, Christina saw something else descending from the ceiling. It was the tigers! They had reappeared and were being lowered to the stage on small circular platforms.

"Come and bow!" the magician commanded. The tigers left their platforms obediently and bowed to Manendra. He patted each on the head and motioned for them to leave the stage.

Christina noticed the tigers were once again very calm. She expected the boy and girl to escort the tigers away, but two men who were not in costumes led them offstage.

"Give me those binoculars!" Christina ordered, before Grant had time to take them off his neck.

"You're choking me!" Grant exclaimed.

"Oh! Sorry, Grant," Christina said.

It was hard to tell with the stage lighting, but as Christina took a closer look at the tigers, they looked different. She had the feeling something wasn't right!

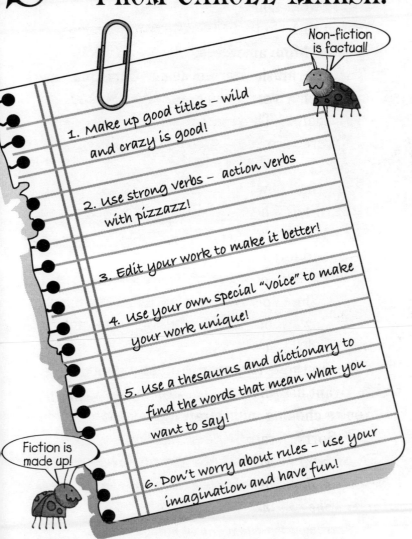

VISIT THE CAROLE MARSH MYSTERIES WEBSITE

www.carolemarshmysteries.com

- *Check out what's coming up next! Are we coming to your area with our next book release? Maybe you can have your book signed by the author!*

- *Join the Carole Marsh Mysteries Fan Club!*

- *Apply for the chance to be a character in an upcoming Carole Marsh Mystery!*

- *Learn how to write your own mystery!*